This Easter book belongs to

....

LADYBIRD BOOKS

UK | USA | Canada | Ireland | Australia | India | New Zealand | South Africa

Ladybird Books is part of the Penguin Random House group of companies whose addresses can be found at global.penguinrandomhouse.com.

www.penguin.co.uk   www.puffin.co.uk   www.ladybird.co.uk

Penguin
Random House
UK

First published 2021
001

Printed in China

A CIP catalogue record for this book is available from the British Library

ISBN: 978-0-241-47640-6

All correspondence to:
Ladybird Books
Penguin Random House Children's
One Embassy Gardens,
8 Viaduct Gardens, London SW11 7BW

Peppa Loves Easter

It was Easter time, and Peppa and her friends were busy making bonnets at playgroup.

"My bonnet has eggs, flowers, feathers and a chocolate muddy puddle!" Peppa said proudly.
"Mine has lots and lots of carrots on it," said Rebecca Rabbit.

"What wonderful bonnets, children!"
cried Madame Gazelle. "Well done!"

After the children put on their bonnets,
Madame Gazelle said, "This Easter, Miss Rabbit
has an egg-citing surprise for you all!"

"Is it an Easter egg hunt?" asked Peppa.
"Not exactly," replied Madame Gazelle.
"But there *are* some eggs."

"Is it an Easter bonnet competition?" asked
Mandy Mouse. "Mine is made of cheese!"

"No, not this year," replied Madame Gazelle. "But you *can* wear your lovely Easter bonnets if you like." "Yippee!" cheered Mandy.

"What *is* the Easter surprise,
Madame Gazelle?" asked Peppa.

"Miss Rabbit has organized an Easter Eggs-travaganza for everyone!" said Madame Gazelle.

"Ooooooh!" gasped the children.

"But what is an Easter . . . Eggsy-travy-ganza, Madame Gazelle?" asked Peppa.
"You'll find out very soon, Peppa!" said Madame Gazelle. "I will be taking you to the Easter Eggs-travaganza after playgroup. Mummy and Daddy Pig are coming to help, too."

"Hooray!" cheered Peppa and her friends.

By the end of the day, all the children were very excited.
"Make sure you take one of these," said Madame Gazelle,
giving them each a little basket to carry. "You'll need them
for the Easter Eggs-travaganza."

"Thank you, Madame Gazelle," cried the children.

"Are you all ready for Miss Rabbit's Easter Eggs-travaganza?" asked Mummy Pig. "Yes!" cried the children, running down the hill.

When they reached the bottom, Peppa, George and their
friends spotted a sign with a cupcake on it.
"*Oooh*, I wonder what that is?" said Daddy Pig in a
mysterious voice. "Shall we follow it?"
"Yes please!" everyone cheered.

The children followed the sign to a stall where they could decorate . . .
"Easter cakes!" gasped Peppa.
"Yummy!" said Daddy Pig.

Everyone had fun decorating the cupcakes,
and then they put them in their baskets.
"But where is Miss Rabbit?" asked Peppa. She looked
around and spotted a sign with an Easter card on it.
"It must be a trail!" she said.

The children followed the trail
until they found lots of lovely
Easter cards to make.

When they finished the cards, they put them in their baskets. "Miss Rabbit isn't here," said Edmond Elephant. "Perhaps we should follow that sign with an egg cup on it?"

The children followed the trail
to an egg-cup-decorating area.

Then, they followed some flower signs to a little meadow full of colourful spring flowers.
"They're so pretty!" gasped Peppa.
"I still can't see Miss Rabbit," said Mandy. "But that sign over there has a little chick on it! Let's go!"

The children followed the trail until they found Granny and
Grandpa Pig . . . and their adorable little chicks!
"Ahhhhhhhh!" cried the children. "They're so fluffy!"
"And so cute!" said Peppa.

"Hello, Peppa," said Granny and Grandpa Pig. "Are
you enjoying Miss Rabbit's Easter Eggs-travaganza?"
"Hello, Granny and Grandpa!" said Peppa. "Yes!
There are so many amazing things to see and do!"

After she had petted every cute little chick, Peppa looked around. "There's a sign with a very big Easter egg on it!" she cried. "This way!"
Peppa and her friends continued along the trail, until . . .

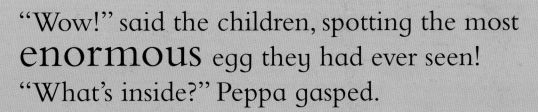

"Wow!" said the children, spotting the most **enormous** egg they had ever seen!
"What's inside?" Peppa gasped.

The children tried to guess what might be inside the enormous egg.

"I think it's a really big carrot!" said Rebecca.

"Dine-saw! Grrr!" roared George.

"It's an alien from Mars!" said Danny Dog.
Suddenly, there was a loud . . .

CRRRRAAACCCKKK!

and out hatched . . .

Miss Rabbit!

"Surprise!" she cried, popping out of the giant egg with treats for everyone. "I hope you enjoyed my Easter Eggs-travaganza!"

"It was egg-cellent!" Daddy Pig chuckled.
"It certainly was!" added Mummy Pig.

Everyone thanked Miss Rabbit for their yummy treats
and for her fantastic Easter Eggs-travaganza.
"Happy Easter, Miss Rabbit!" cheered Peppa and her friends.
"Happy Easter, children!" said Miss Rabbit.

Peppa loves Easter.
Everyone loves Easter!